Fallout
Living in the Shadow of the Bomb

Kara,

Thankyou very much
for your support of the
BNTVA my purchasing this book.

Sarah Moron.

First Printing: 2018
ISBN 978-1-9164785-1-0

Also available for Kindle from Amazon.

For all information contact Mr Slaine McRoth via email:
slainemcroth@yahoo.com

Fallout

Living in the Shadow of the Bomb

Clifford Jones

Edited by Slaine McRoth

Published by Slaine McRoth

2018

Contents

A Note from the Editor

I received this manuscript from Frederick Jones. He gave me his story to enable the BNTVA – British Nuclear Test Veterans Association – to promote the struggles of everyday life for many of the families of the nuclear testing programme veterans. I do not know if this story is a true account of his family's struggles, but through my research and discussions with the descendants of nuclear veterans, I believe it is representative of their combined stories. Every day families still live with the legacy of the nuclear testing programmes across the world. I hope this story will encourage other descendants to join their respective associations and continue the recognition campaigns. This is Frederick's story.

Slaine McRoth

Introduction

My name is Frederick Jones and I am the son of a British nuclear veteran. This book has been compiled from my father's memoirs, which I discovered after my mother's death in 2017. The memoirs, which my mother continued to update after my father's death, had been kept secret from my siblings and me.

My father committed suicide 16 years after he witnessed the Grapple series of explosions on Christmas Island in 1958. I have added to the memoirs and, after reading *The X, Y and Z Files* by Slaine McRoth, I contacted the author and asked him if he would help me publish this book so that families who are suffering because of their father's or grandfather's participation at nuclear tests across the world would realise they are not alone.

My father did not talk to me about his time on Christmas Island; he kept it very private. It was only after discovering his memoir that I realised how much my mother knew about his experiences. I now understand she was well aware of the problems he was having but did her best to protect my siblings and me. I'm so grateful she continued to update the memoir after his death, so the story of our family is complete.

Words cannot describe how much my family has been affected by the nuclear testing programme carried out by the UK Government. Even though my father witnessed the tests before I was born, it's had a huge effect on my life. I have lived through many years of doubt, depression and anger and wonder if there will ever be a time when the UK Government will acknowledge the sacrifice of these brave men, who gave so much to ensure Britain had nuclear capabilities.

If my father had not witnessed these tests, my life may have been very different. He was a Chief Petty Officer in the Royal Navy and in civilian life may have captained commercial ships. We will never know just how successful he may have been because in January 1974, on New Year's Day, he committed suicide. I was 12 years old. My sister Elizabeth was 14; my older brother David, who died two years earlier, would have been 16.

My mother passed away from cancer in 2017; she was 79. She never recovered from losing her eldest son and her husband in such a short space of time. These tests changed our family forever. We are still experiencing health issues.

The many studies that have been carried out by the UK Government have concluded that the tests did not irradiate the personnel and did not contribute towards the cancers and illnesses that the personnel and their families experienced. I do not know how they can deny this. I am a member of the Fallout Group on Facebook (a closed group run by the BNTVA) and when discussing illness and health issues, a common pattern emerges. The percentage of descendants affected is much higher than the general population. To be ignored by the UK Government is a disgrace – and one which we must fight to rectify.

The British Nuclear Test Veterans Association continues to fight for recognition for these veterans and their latest medal campaign has raised awareness of the veterans and their families. The board of trustees works very hard to ensure that we are not forgotten. When I read stories of the suffering of the families and the denial of any wrongdoing by the UK Government, it makes me so angry. Studies on health and wellbeing have been carried out by Dr Becky Martin under the NCCF Nuclear Families project, but it needs more in-depth analysis. These tests could still be affecting 150,000 people today. Why are we ignored?

I saw a picture of a US veteran wearing a T-shirt saying: "Deny, Delay Until We Die." It sums up the UK Government's attitude and their constant denials.

The NCCF are funding research at Brunel University into the DNA changes affecting the children of veterans. Hopefully this will prove that the veterans were exposed, their DNA was altered and that this has been passed on to their children. This important research may finally stop the denials. Let's hope that it does.

Please do not feel sorry for my family. We had many happy times together and lots of laughter and I have fond memories of my father. This book, which details the struggles he went through, is full of sadness but he provided for us and I still believe he took his own life in order to protect us from his demons.

Chapter 1 – This is Me: Clifford Jones (Jonesy)

If you are reading these memoirs, then I have finally succeeded in killing myself. These notes are all that is left of my life. I am truly sorry that I could no longer live with the guilt and the pressures of everyday life. To my wife May, I did not want to burden you with this life – with three children with health problems that I believe are due to my participation at the British nuclear tests. I never wanted to leave you – you are my world – but if I do not go now, I cannot guarantee that I will not harm you and the children. You are better off without me. Please do not see me as a coward. I am trying to protect you and what remains of our family.

My name is Clifford David Jones and I was born on the 20th September 1936 in Salisbury. Times were hard when I was growing up; we did not have much, but I had a happy childhood. My father was a farmer, and I was lucky to have fresh produce and milk on the table every day. Many of my friends did not have such luxuries.

I grew up on the farm and was soon fixing tractors and machines and helping my father to tend the land and keep the animals. Farm life was hard work and I did not go to school as much as I should have. I wanted to be an officer in the Royal Navy and whenever I could I researched boats and built models from wood left around the farm. My father encouraged me at every opportunity, but he reminded me that the farm came first and that I must always provide a roof over my family's head and food on the table. Everything else was a luxury. As long as you had a dry place to lay your head and your family were provided for, you could be content and happy.

I desperately wanted to join the navy and when I was 16, I decided to sign up for the service. My father refused to sign my papers. Instead, he sold half his farm to pay for me to go to boarding school for two years. "If you want to become an officer, you must have an education," he said. "Your brothers can look after the farm. You must follow your dreams and study hard."

At the time, I was devastated. I wanted to join immediately, but with no formal qualifications, I was never to become a navigator. My father was right: I needed an education. For those two years I studied as hard as I possibly could and on my 18th birthday, I enrolled in the Royal Navy. It was 1954 and the armed forces were still recovering from the Second World War. Navy officers were scarce and the recruitment process for new officers was well underway. I enrolled to become a navigator and was sent to Portsmouth for my training.

Having spent two years at boarding school I was now used to being away from home and living in dormitories, but I was not prepared for the navy lifestyle. The training was hard, the food was awful and after three months I wrote home to ask for permission to leave. My father wrote back to tell me it would be the worst decision of my life if I left. He wanted me to succeed. I often wonder how different my life would have been if I had left the navy. I definitely know I would not be sitting here with a shotgun on my lap, considering killing myself.

My family do not know of these memoirs, these night-time writings that keep me sane. My children do not know of the daily battle that I have every time I see them struggle with their health. I blame myself. Every day I look at David's picture in my wallet and want to kill myself. His life was cut so short. His wonderful smile and infectious laugh still haunt me. Why did the UK Government allow me to be used as a guinea pig in these awful tests? Why did they deny any responsibility? How could the Queen allow her subjects to be treated this way?

Chapter 2 – How It Started

I met May in July 1957. She was the prettiest girl I had ever seen. I was a bit of a rogue, fighting and drinking, and she was the complete opposite. She had jet black hair and was the girl for me.

We met on a double date. I was going out with her friend at the time, but I knew as soon as I saw her that I was going to spend the rest of my life with her. I was already in the navy and she was working for a pharmaceutical company. We just clicked. Her mother told her to watch out for me. "He has a bad reputation," she said. My father told me that she was not right for me. We didn't care.

She lived in Swindon and I was stationed at Whale Island, Portsmouth. We kept in contact via letter and every time I had leave, I would come home and visit her. We would dance the night away, drink and have fun. Life could not get any better. I had my career, my girl and my whole life in front of me.

I was involved in the preparation of ships for the Grapple series of explosions on Christmas Island; we also prepared aircraft as "Sniffers" for the explosions. I did not know anything about radiation or nuclear bombs. We had a job to do and I was privileged to be involved. My main role was to find a suitable course across the island and to navigate the monitoring ship before and after the dropping of the bombs. I never envisaged that I would actually be going to Christmas Island myself.

I received my posting at the beginning of April 1958. My role was to be a navigator for the main drop of Grapple Y. I was given four days' leave before I left for a six-month posting. I was enthusiastic about leaving the UK for the first time and on discovering the island was a Pacific paradise, I was even more excited. My only concern was leaving May. We had talked about getting engaged and married, and six months away from her would be excruciating.

During my leave I decided I would propose to her, so she would remain my girl whilst I was away. I took May to Salisbury Plain for a picnic under the moonlight. I asked her to marry me and she said yes. I told her about my posting to Christmas Island. She was intrigued; she wanted to know where the island was, did they receive post, how hot was it and why was I going?

I informed her that I was to help navigate a ship across the island for a bomb test, but I was sworn to secrecy about the nature of the bomb. When I look back now, I did not know anything about the bomb that the plane was carrying. I did not question the payload, the effects or any aspect of the test.

I assured May that I would be fine: I was just monitoring the bomb, nothing else. In fact, I believed that I was to be in a privileged position. After all, there were thousands of personnel on the island at ground level and I would be at sea.

That night was probably the best night of my life. I am so glad I proposed as May was the best wife a man could ask for and a fantastic mother to our children.

Chapter 3 – My Involvement in The Tests

As I was the navigator in my crew my tasks were: to ensure the ship was positioned correctly to allow for the monitoring of the bomb; to ensure we were in the correct position at the correct time; and to ensure that we were far enough away when the bomb dropped that we were not in harm's way.

I spent weeks planning the bomb drop, co-ordinating the drop with maps and charts to ensure it was carried out to perfection.

I arrived on the island on April 14th 1958. My calculations were checked by the scientists and we were in agreement that the plane would drop the bomb and then would be given enough time to fly a safe distance from the explosion. I was to have the best view of the explosion from the monitoring ship, or so I thought.

A week later, I was summoned to my Commanding Officer. My duties and those of the monitoring ships had changed. We were to be closer to the explosion than we first thought. The scientists had recalibrated the bomb and we needed to change our calculations and navigation charts. I immediately took on this duty with no thought as to my safety. My navigation skills and mapping of the island was invaluable to the mission. We needed to be closer to the explosion, but not too close as to put the ship in danger.

This single incident was to change my life forever. It is strange when I look back and think about tragedies in my life. Parents dying, children dying, your first pet dying. These are all major events. But this single change to my duty has affected the life of my family and will do so for generations.

I lie awake at night and think "Why?" What would have happened if we had not been asked to get closer to the explosion? Would I be suffering these terrible headaches? Would my son have died so young? I will never know the answers to these questions. But I want to know. Is there a parallel universe where another version of me is living without these issues, where my son is still alive and is fit and healthy?

On April 28th 1958, Grapple Y was dropped at 19:05 UK time. I witnessed the largest explosion ever carried out by the UK Government. It was a fantastic sight, but one I would never want anyone to see again. The image is etched on my brain.

To this day, I cannot bear to hear a countdown. I watched the launch of the Apollo missions, but the take-off countdown brought back floods of memories, memories that were too painful. I try to block out the images, but they continue to haunt me. I know I will never be free of the images. I try and replace them with pictures of my family, but the picture of my dead son is the only one I see.

I wore no protective clothing, just my uniform. Dosimeters were placed around our ship with a large amount of monitoring equipment. I was told that they were monitoring the radiation levels to ensure that we were 'safe'. Little did I know that we were being used as guinea pigs in a large experiment. The ship was so 'hot' after the explosion that only a few personnel were allowed on deck. I was to supervise the cleaning of the ship. We pumped water from the sea onto the ship's deck until the readings were at a 'safe' level. I had to endure five showers until the Geiger counters told the scientists we were safe to leave.

You have to remember that I was only 22; we had no radiation training, knew nothing about exposure risk and we were told nothing about the dangers. I was just serving my country.

Chapter 4 – Sent Home Due to Illness

Twenty-four hours after the explosion, I was asked to decontaminate the ship again. For a second time we pumped radioactive water onto the ship and cleansed the decks.

The next day, I started to be violently sick. I had eaten supper and believed that my sickness was caused by food poisoning, it was that severe. It was at this time that I first experienced the worst headache of my life. It was a migraine of extreme proportions; I felt as if my brain was going to explode.

I hoped this would be an isolated incident and that once I was well enough, I would be able to return to duties. I stayed in the hospital for two weeks, still being violently sick and experiencing excruciating pain in my head.

It was during this stay that I first encountered the lies and deceit of the UK Government. I was given lots of tests and numerous doctors prodded and poked me. Blood and urine samples were taken and I was given intravenous drugs via a drip. I was told that I was dehydrated and needed the drip to ensure my fluid levels were maintained. By this point, I was so ill that I honestly believed I was going to die. I floated in and out of consciousness. Even though I was barely conscious, I kept seeing the same person at the end of my bed. At first, I thought he was a doctor, but he seemed more like a scientist. He would discuss my progress with the doctors and record information relating to me. During one visit, I pretended to be asleep and overheard them talking about my exposure levels and that the dosimeter readings were "off the scale". It was at this point that I suspected I had been exposed to high levels of radiation.

After two weeks, I stopped being sick and started to feel better. Perhaps it had been a severe case of food poisoning after all. I assumed that I would return to my duties on the island for the remainder of my six-month posting but on May 13th, I was told that I would be returning home for an extended period of leave. No reason was given, and I was glad to be off the island. Conditions were bearable at the best of times;

land crabs and tents were the best I could hope for if I stayed.

I was to return to the UK via Hawaii and was given six weeks' leave. I could return to May and recuperate with my bride-to-be. I was thrilled to be going home.

Before I left the island, one of my colleagues asked me what my rash was. "Are you allergic? You need to stop eating the crabs!" he joked. I hadn't noticed it before, but my body was covered in a rash, especially around my testicles. My potential bride would think I had been up to no good!

I returned home to Salisbury. When May saw me, she started to cry. "What have they done to you?" she sobbed. I had lost 30 pounds and was covered in a strange rash. "We need to get you to Bob," she said. Her brother, Bob, was a doctor with his own general practice.

Bob checked me over and was intrigued by the rash. When I told him what I had been involved with on the island, he said he believed the rash was radiation poisoning. He had never seen it before, but he was convinced that I had it.

You have to remember that this was in the late 1950s, when we did not have access to photographs and he could only consult the medical journals for his diagnosis.

May and I decided to get married during my six weeks of leave. We were married on 1st July and we were to live in married quarters in Portsmouth. We went to the Isle of Wight for our honeymoon and it was during this trip that our first son was conceived.

We moved into the married quarters and my career within the navy continued. My first son was born on 20th February 1959 and we named him David, after his uncle. He was a healthy weight (7 pounds 8 ounces) but his breathing was not right.

Chapter 5 – My RAF Career

I continued my navy career and was promoted through the ranks to Chief Petty Officer. I was earning a good wage and we now had three children. David was joined by Elizabeth and Fred. All were suffering health problems.

As a Chief Petty Officer, we were housed in good accommodation, my children were attending a good school and we were saving for the future. May and I discussed purchasing our own house when I left the navy and we had accumulated enough savings to buy a property.

It was at this time that my father died. This was a devastating blow to the family; the farm was my parents' main source of income. I did not want to return to the farming life, so my brother took on the farm, so he could provide for his family.

However, May and I decided to purchase the farm next door. We moved my mother into the new farmhouse and my brother farmed the land. This farm would be our pension when I left the navy.

The headaches continued throughout my time in the navy. They were worse when I was at sea and the air pressure was constantly changing. Eventually, I was grounded on medical advice. I was spending more time experiencing headaches than not.

By now I was an instructor and had not sailed in any capacity for over five years. My children were growing up fast and I needed to decide whether to continue my career in the navy or start a new career in civilian life.

The navy life was all I had known as an adult; I had moved from the farm to boarding school to the navy. If I was to become a civilian, what would be my trade? Under normal circumstances, I would work in the commercial airline sector, but my headaches prevented me from flying.

I started to miss more classes than I was teaching. My headaches were getting worse. I was starting to have severe mood swings and it was having an effect on the family unit. I was not sleeping at night; insomnia was my enemy. The children asked me to help with homework and to attend their extra-curricular activities, but I could not stand to be anywhere noisy. Any loud music caused me great pain and I started to retreat into one room within our married quarters.

My only solace was my pipe. I smoked a lot during those days as it seemed to soothe the effects of the headaches.

Eventually, I was called to my Commanding Officer, who demanded I undertake a full medical to ascertain what the issues were with my health. It was February 1970 and I was no longer able to carry out my duties. I knew that I was going to be medically discharged, and I discussed the situation with May.

We had the farm and the family back in Salisbury. My mother was still alive, fit and healthy and would help with the children if May and I had to work. I did not resign from the navy; I awaited the medical discharge to enable us to have a pay-out which would allow the family to relocate.

Without the farm, we would have been in trouble. My father had been right all along: keep a roof over your head and food on the table. What else did we need?

Chapter 6 – The Children

Of the three children in our family, Fred is the healthiest. He seems to have no major health issues, apart from very soft teeth. Elizabeth has many problems, most prominently eyesight issues as she has only 30% sight.

David is our main concern. He has struggled with severe asthma and breathing difficulties. He is constantly ill, and we hate the winters as this is when he struggles the most. Any cold turns into a chest infection and he spends weeks in bed recovering.

At first, I did not attribute any of my children's illnesses to my participation at the tests. I did not make any connection. I did, however, believe that I had been affected by the tests. Before I went to the island I did not suffer any headaches but after my exposure I experienced daily issues.

In the 1960s, we did not understand any link between children's illness and family conditions. My doctor asked me if other members of my family had suffered asthma and breathing problems, but I could not recall any problems. My father was a fit, healthy farmer who had died following a farming accident. My mother was still alive and had no health concerns.

David was in and out of hospital on a regular basis. Elizabeth attended Moorfields Eye Hospital for surgery to fix astigmatism and to colour her eye. Fred has undergone numerous dental appointments to remove teeth that have not formed.

Specialists have told us that Elizabeth's eyesight will continue to deteriorate and that she will need regular checks and could eventually lose her sight completely. May is devastated; she cannot understand why Elizabeth's sight is so bad. Elizabeth has a very rare condition which has affected her since birth yet there is no history of this in the family on either side. The specialists are intrigued about what has caused this issue and the continued degeneration of her eyes.

David's condition continues to worsen each year. He desperately wants to play football, but his asthma is so severe he struggles to breathe when performing any exercise. I sit and listen to him wheezing and coughing and want to trade places with him. No parent should listen to their child suffer and to see all three children having problems breaks my heart.

May is the one I worry about the most; she is nursing her young children. She cries nearly every night and I do not comfort her. My headaches are so severe that I sit in my rocking chair, smoking my pipe when the children have gone to bed. Everyone except May is ill and she and I have started arguing.

Our household is not a happy place. I am under intense pressure at work to complete training courses for the new recruits. I am also under pressure from my wife to help her with the children. My children want my attention and I cannot provide for them because of these severe headaches.

The children do not want to leave the navy structure. They are worried that if we move back to Salisbury, they will lose their friends and the comfortable life we have at the moment will cease to exist. Fred does not want to live on the farm.

I am struggling with what to do for my children and my wife. Perhaps they would be better off without me in their lives. If I cannot provide for them, what is my role? What is my purpose?

Chapter 7 – Discharge from the Navy

In May 1970, 16 years after joining the Royal Navy, I was medically discharged. My final rank was Chief Petty Officer. I was given a pay-out and we moved the family to Salisbury from Portsmouth.

My children did not want to move from the safety net that the navy provided for them. They would need to start again at new schools and make new friends. I was the enemy at this time.

May was brilliant during my discharge. She arranged everything, from moving our possessions to changing the children's schools and ensuring that the move went smoothly.

Unfortunately, my headaches became much worse during the transition from the navy to civilian life. The stress on the family was immense. I had no profession and was now spending days in bed in a dark room, unable to function.

It was at this point that my depression started to take hold. For anyone who has experienced depression, it is one of the most terrible experiences you can have. Add to this excruciating headaches and not being able to lift your head off the pillow and you have a recipe for disaster.

For the first few months back on the farm, life was terrible. The children did not transition to the new school very well and Elizabeth was bullied because of her eye condition. May was struggling with the children and looking after me.

It was a visit from my mother that started my recovery. She came to visit me when no one else was in the house. She sat by the side of my bed with a photo album and showed me pictures of her and my father when they first purchased the farm. My father had both his legs in casts.

She explained that my father had broken his legs falling from the barn whilst hay bailing. He had to spend six weeks in plaster and could not tend the farm. I knew nothing of this, as it happened before I was born. She explained that she had to tend to the farm, look after her husband and ensure they had food on the table. She told me that if I did not get out of bed, there would be no one to provide for my family.

She told me I needed to see a doctor and get help. New drugs were coming onto the market that could help me. She'd arranged for the family doctor to visit the farm and he'd be arriving in 10 minutes. I was to wash, shave and make myself presentable. The family name depended on it.

My mother's words made me realise I could get up, I could help May and I could provide for my family. I washed and shaved for the first time in weeks. The doctor prescribed me with strong painkillers to help with the headaches and anti-depressants. I was to take them daily and report back to him in two weeks' time.

When May and the children returned home, I was dressed and preparing a meal in the kitchen. I was in a positive frame of mind and determined to get a job to provide for my family.

I started the hunt for a job. I was prepared to do anything to ensure my family was provided for. I applied for a job at an engineering firm in Salisbury who were building new navigational equipment and wanted an experienced navigator to ensure the instruments they were developing were correctly configured. Because of my navy experience, I was given the position. Once again, my father had been right. I could still provide for my family.

The painkillers were working, and the anti-depressants were allowing me to stay positive. The children had settled in their new schools and were starting to make friends. May and I were sleeping in the same bed and had made love for the first time in months. My life was back on track and for the first time in years, I felt positive. The nightmare visions of the nuclear explosions were starting to fade.

Unfortunately, this period of happiness was short-lived. David had started to develop complications and his condition was deteriorating.

Chapter 8 – David's Illnesses

In May 1971, David began to experience severe breathing difficulties. He could not walk a few steps without struggling for breath.

He was admitted to hospital and they ran numerous tests on him. His small pale body looked so frail as he lay on the bed.

Initially asthma was blamed for his condition. He was given stronger and stronger inhalers. Nothing worked.

In July 1971, he collapsed at school and was rushed by ambulance to Salisbury Hospital. I was working in Salisbury and immediately went to his bedside. When I entered the room where he lay, I thought he was dead. His breathing was shallow, his skin translucent. There were large bruises on his arms where he had fallen and a cut across his nose where he had hit it on the floor.

Further tests were undertaken, and May and I were visited by a specialist who gave us the diagnosis. Our 13-year-old son had lung cancer. May began crying hysterically. It was not possible. He was 13 years old. How could this have happened?

I was numb with the news. In my mind I tried to block it out. There was no way this could happen. My beautiful son. Then it hit me like an express train. My exposure at the nuclear tests. Had I caused this? Was I responsible for my son's condition?

I asked the specialist if my exposure could have anything to do with the cancer. He dismissed it immediately and told me it was not connected. I was not convinced. Radiation exposure was not something the doctors were specialised in.

I was not in contact with any of my colleagues from the tests, so I had no one to talk to, to see if they were experiencing similar issues with their health or their children.

The next question I asked the specialist was the hardest one I would ever ask. "How long does he have?" I was told that further tests would be needed but it would be under 12 months.

Just as my life was turning around, it was blown apart. No parent should ever watch their child die. May and I discussed David and we agreed that we would not tell the other children. We would tell them that he had to stay in hospital, but we would not give them the full diagnosis.

It was extremely hard to return to the farm and not break down. We had three children and we needed to keep the family together. May was very strong, but I heard her crying outside. She had gone into the barn so that no one would see her.

David remained in hospital for a while and then returned home. His condition had worsened, and we were told that the fast approaching Christmas would be his last. We decided to make it a fun experience; we would not allow his illness to stop the family enjoying Christmas. I took a leave of absence from work; my bosses understood the situation.

We threw the best party ever. Other family members attended, and we ensured that everyone had a great time. We saw in the New Year with David sitting with me in the rocking chair. I knew he had only months to live. He had little breath and his speech was limited, but as I was rocking him, he whispered: "Thank you, Dad, this Christmas has been the best one yet." I smiled at him and told him we had many more to come.

This was the hardest thing I had ever done. Lying to your dying child is something that no one should ever have to do. His smile when I replied will stay with me for the rest of my life.

David remained at home until his death on 13th March 1972. He was 14 years old. He died peacefully with his mother and me at his side. He took his last breath at 11 in the morning. It was a beautiful day; the sun was shining, and I remember the cows were in the field under his bedroom window.

I sat with him until the undertakers arrived. The doctor had certified his death and there was to be a post mortem as he was a minor who had died at home. The hour that passed was the longest hour I have ever experienced. I sat and talked to him; I held his hand: he was still warm to the touch and it looked as if he was sleeping.

Anyone who has experienced losing a child knows you never get over it. You stay strong for the rest of the family, but it stays with you forever.

When the undertakers arrived, I helped them take his body out of the house. I did not want to leave him. He was gone, but I did not want him to go. It was after the undertaker left that my anger and rage started. I was convinced that my exposure to radiation had caused his cancer. How could a 14-year-old boy die from lung cancer? It must be connected. It was my fault. I had contributed to my own son's death.

Chapter 9 – The Funeral

David's funeral was to be held on 27th March 1972, a church service with a burial in Salisbury Cemetery. This was the hardest day of my life.

May had arranged the funeral, chosen the hymns and arranged the service. I could not bring myself to get involved. My depression had returned, and the headaches had started again.

I retreated to my chair and pipe and started going out to the barn to chop wood to vent my anger with the situation. I wanted my son back. I would give my life if I could to allow him to live. I knew that he could never come back, but I wanted it more than anything in the world.

May had requested that people did not dress in black but wore colourful clothes, as David had done during his short life. Everywhere I looked, the image of him in my arms smiling at me came into my mind. He had so much to live for, his whole life in front of him, and for no fault of his own it had been cruelly taken away.

I could not cope on the day; I was a mess. The other children were dressed, and May was shouting at me to get dressed and attend my son's funeral. Those words "son's funeral" resonated in my head. Then I had a vision of my father, telling me to provide for my family. I was the head of the family and I could not allow May to take the full burden of the funeral. I had to be strong.

I dressed quickly and stood with my family as the hearse containing my son's body came to the farm. There he was, in a wooden box, taking his last ride in a car. My emotions were in overdrive and my headache was at an excruciating level. I had to get through it.

I do not remember the ceremony; it was a blur. It was as if I was watching a TV drama. This was not real life; it was a nightmare that I would wake up from. After the ceremony, family and friends attended the graveside and we watched as the coffin was lowered into the ground. It was at this point that I lost control of my mind and tried to throw myself into the grave after David's coffin. My brother stopped me and restrained me. I was distraught and experiencing my first breakdown.

After the burial, a wake was held at a local community centre. Everyone was very polite and respectful, but I knew what they were all thinking: "Thank God this hasn't happened to me." I blamed myself. I blamed the UK Government.

The children went to bed early as they were exhausted. May and I sat at the kitchen table and for the first time, she raised the subject of the nuclear testing programme and asked me if I thought it was connected. She had never mentioned the tests before. I told her I didn't know, there had been no research. I was not in contact with other test veterans, so I had no idea.

This was the first time May hit me. She was so upset that she broke down and took her anger out on me, punching and punching my chest, saying: "The tests did this!" over and over again.

Eventually she stopped and asked me to explain what tasks I had performed at the tests. She wanted to know everything. She wanted justice for her son. We sat and talked until 4am and I told her everything I could remember.

Life was difficult for the next few months. The children were subdued and the family did not know what to say to us. We visited David's grave and talked to him. I was determined he would not be forgotten.

Chapter 10 – My First Suicide Attempt

In June 1972, I attempted suicide for the first time. The loss of my son was too much for me to bear. My headaches were so severe that I had taken to lying in the barn under a blanket, away from the noise of the house and any human contact.

May was struggling to cope with the other children. On numerous occasions she broke down and I was unable to comfort her.

I was a failure. I had not been able to save my son. I was not providing for my family either; I had taken so much time off work that they had asked me to leave my job.

May had taken a part time job in the local shop and we were living off her income, savings and my mother's pension.

I was spending more and more time alone, in the barn, or wandering around the field. My depression was at its highest level. I contemplated killing the whole family so we could all be with David. If he could not live, then we should all die so we could be together.

This idea came more and more each day. Perhaps I should just kill myself. May could look after the other two children and I could be with David. Was I being selfish? My relationship with May was at a low point. I was not sleeping with her, I was not communicating with her, we were just existing.

I went to visit David's grave and sat for two hours and talked to him. I convinced myself that he wanted me to be with him. If I died, I could protect him and ensure he was safe.

I decided to end my life that night, in the barn. I had a shotgun and I could shoot myself. If I did it in the barn, there would be no mess in the house and May could prevent the kids from seeing me.

May had prepared tea when I returned. I took it to the barn and ate alone. I waited for the children to go to bed and then returned the plate and cup. May was in the kitchen, washing the dishes. She still looked as beautiful as the first day I set eyes upon her.

I do not know why, but I went to her and gave her a hug and kissed her and told her that I loved her and the children. She was shocked as I had not had any physical contact with her since David's death. Then I told her I had been to visit David and that I would be visiting him again soon.

I kissed her again and said I had to clean my gun and I was going to the barn to do it. She looked into my eyes and said, "I love you." I told her I loved her too and went out to the barn.

I had prepared bales of hay in such a way that once I pulled the trigger, I would fall into the hay and any blood would be soaked up. The moment had come. I sat on the hay bales and brought the barrels of the gun up to my mouth. "I will be with you soon, David," I said. I was about to pull the trigger when I saw May standing in front of me.

"Don't you dare!" she said. "You have two other children in that house. They need a father more than ever now."

I was shocked by her tone. It was as if she was telling off a puppy who had stolen food from the table. I dropped the gun and went over to her. She hugged me and told me that she loved me.

"We need to work together to get through this. Talk to me, open up with me. The other children need us," she said. I cried and cried. What had my life come to? A promising navy officer with a beautiful wife and family. Now I was standing in a barn, about to blow my brains out after burying my son. I needed help.

May and I sat down and discussed the desperate situation. We were both hurting from our son's death, but we had two other children who needed our love and support. I agreed to visit the doctor the next morning.

I attended the doctor's surgery and explained the situation and he suggested that I was referred to a psychiatrist so I could get specialist advice.

I quickly received an appointment. I was desperate to speak to a professional who could help me. My first appointment was a difficult one. I found it very hard to talk to anyone about my feelings. I was a member of Her Majesty's Armed Forces; we didn't do such things.

The psychiatrist asked me about my childhood, my upbringing and schooling. I told him I'd had a happy childhood and was privileged to attend a boarding school.

It was when we discussed my time on Christmas Island that he became interested. We concentrated on this aspect of my life as he firmly believed that I was suffering from traumatic stress from my time at the tests. He told me that my records did not mention the exposure levels and, more importantly, they did not mention that I had changed duties and moved closer to the explosion. It was as if I was a forgotten man.

The subject of my son's death and the attempted suicide were discussed, and he gave me stronger anti-depressants and recommended that I attend five further sessions so we could discuss my life in greater detail.

I attended two further sessions. My mood was improving, I had another job, which was keeping me busy, and my headaches were less severe. It was during the fourth visit that the doctor informed me he had discovered the amount of radiation I had been exposed to. It was the equivalent of having 12,000 X-rays in 24 hours. My head and testicles had been especially exposed.

He was preparing a report for the government and my GP so I could be flagged as having high level exposure. I had the result I wanted: the exposure had caused my headaches and affected my testicles. And as a result, my children had been born with health issues; it was, inadvertently, my fault.

The day before my fifth visit, I received a letter from the doctor's surgery informing me that my final two appointments with the psychiatrist had been cancelled. They told me I had made sufficient progress that the last two sessions were not necessary. I never saw the psychiatrist again.

I did visit my GP for a routine appointment and asked him if my files had been flagged for radiation exposure. He looked through the notes and told me he could find no details or reports from the psychiatrist. I was puzzled. The psychiatrist had told me he had found my exposure readings and was preparing a report and I would finally have closure.

I telephoned the psychiatrist's practice and was told that the doctor had left the practice and there were no notes relating to my case, apart from those which had been passed on to my GP.

Chapter 11 – More Issues

For the next few months, life improved. We never forgot David; we just got on with life. Our two children needed help at school and with football and hockey. I was happy at work and became the taxi driver for my children's activities.

It was now September 1972. I was watching Fred play football when I had an inkling something was not right at home. A feeling of dread overcame me. I didn't think anything of it though. Fred finished his game and we returned home to the farm. When I approached the drive, I saw an ambulance in the driveway. What had happened now? Just as my life was getting back on track, another issue had arisen.

When I got to the house, May was at the door, crying, with Elizabeth. "It's your mother," she said. "She's suffered a stroke." I rushed upstairs to her room, where she was lying on the bed. She couldn't talk. She tried to smile, but the left side of her face refused to move; it was as if the left side of her face had melted.

The ambulance crew explained that they were taking her into hospital for tests as they could not tell how much damage the stroke had caused. I held her hand and told her everything would be OK and that she would recover. Mother tried to smile at me and I saw David's face as it had been on New Year's Eve. History had repeated itself, and I was again trying to protect a family member.

My life was to be turned upside down once again. My mother never returned home. After looking into my eyes for one last time, she lost consciousness and died three days later – in the same hospital where David had died.

May took control of the family again. I was a mess; the hard work in the psychiatric sessions had been undone in an instant. Was this family cursed? Why were we experiencing these tragedies? I retreated to my pipe and to the barn once again, spending long hours alone with my demons, which had returned stronger than ever.

On the day of my mother's funeral, I awoke in the barn with the worst headache I had ever had. It was as if a sledgehammer was pounding on the inside of my skull, and when I stood, I felt dizzy. I had not eaten for days and looked terrible. I smelt, my hair was unbrushed and my clothes were like rags.

May came into the barn and saw the terrible state I was in. The funeral was in three hours. "We need to make you presentable," she said. She cut my hair, washed it, washed me and presented me with clean underwear and a newly pressed suit. "You need to make her proud."

My mother had always been there for me. She had got me through my initial depression and she would not want to see me like this. I needed to pull myself together. I took extra painkillers and stepped out with my family. The funeral was a simple service and we buried her in the same cemetery as David.

The painkillers numbed the headache, so I started to take more tablets each day. The headaches never went away fully, but with the extra painkillers, they were now bearable. I returned to work and life went on.

Christmas came. We spent time together as a family. We visited David, and my mother and father. They were now together in peace and I asked my parents to look after my son.

1973 started well. I was promoted at work, the children were doing well at school and Fred had been selected to represent the county at football. To the outside world, we were the perfect family: we appeared to have two perfect children, a large farm, good jobs and were very happy. But things were still not right between May and me. Whilst we had resumed sleeping in the same bed, we had not made love for nearly a year.

I was taking more and more painkillers, buying further tablets and adding them to my prescription. It was at this time that I decided to stop smoking. The health effects of smoking were becoming more prominent in the press and I wanted to show May that I was committed to our marriage. She had always hated smoking, so I did it for her.

Unfortunately, I replaced nicotine with alcohol. It started with a bottle of wine with dinner; May and I shared the bottle and enjoyed it together. This led to two bottles and before I knew it, I was drinking wine for breakfast. I hid it from May, but she knew I was coping by using drugs and alcohol.

Chapter 12 – My Second Suicide Attempt

In August 1973, I was driving to work when I was involved in a road traffic accident. I was rear-ended in a traffic jam by another car, forcing me into the car in front. I did not suffer any major physical injuries, but I was breathalysed at the scene and found to be two times over the limit. It was 8 am when I was tested.

I was arrested and charged with driving under the influence of alcohol. I was bailed and returned to the farm. The car insurance refused to pay out because I had been charged. When the person who hit me found out, they changed their story and I was informed that I had also been charged with dangerous driving, as it was claimed that I lost control of the car and braked suddenly.

I protested my innocence but lost the court case. In December 1973, I was banned from driving and lost my job, as I needed a driving licence to carry out my duties. Again, life had kicked me when I was down.

May returned to work to enable us to live day to day. We were burning through our savings and I sold various items of memorabilia and farm equipment to make ends meet. Christmas was to be a torrid affair: we had no money to buy the presents that the children wanted, and I did not even have enough to buy May a present.

I walked into the barn and looked at the tractor that my family had used on the farm for generations. I had no choice but to sell my final memory of my father. We needed to pay the mortgage on the farm, buy Christmas presents. I sold the tractor at a knock down price and bought presents for the children and a new ring for May.

I had provided for my family, and we spent Christmas at home, exchanging gifts. May was depressed, but her face lit up when she saw the ring. It was as if she was 14 years younger, on Salisbury Plain, and I was proposing to her.

Over the Christmas holidays, May and I made love a number of times. She was looking forward to the new year and another new start. I promised to get a job and help her with the bills and the children. We saw in the new year together and she went to bed.

Chapter 13 – The End

I sat in my rocking chair with a bottle of whiskey, considering the future and how we needed to rebuild our family life. The painkillers and the whiskey were keeping my headache at bay, but I was now starting to doubt myself.

My mother and father were dead. I had no support network, no one to talk to. My psychiatrist had been removed from my case. I was the head of the family and I had failed to save my son.

The image of him sitting with me on the rocking chair came into my mind. It was as if he was sitting on my lap. Then came an image of my mother with her face melting, then my father telling me to be the strong person, be a man. Provide for your family.

I can't do it.

I wrote this entry in my memoir, not intending it to be my last; however, I feel it might be. I now have my shotgun. The voices in my head are telling me to kill May and the children and then myself to stop the misery.

If we are all dead, we can all be together.

The shotgun is double barrelled, so I will only have two shots. It will be quick if I shoot the children, then May. No, perhaps it would be better to kill May, then reload and kill the children.

What am I thinking? Where has this come from? I cannot kill my own family.

There is no other option. If I continue to drink and take the painkillers, I will not be able to provide for my family. If they are with me, I will be able to look after them in the afterlife.

I must stop thinking these thoughts.

I decided to lock the shotgun in the gun cabinet and threw away the key into the fields next to the barn. This way I can't shoot them. I returned to my rocking chair and drank more whiskey. I had saved the family from death. I could not shoot them. I looked at the kitchen knives on the draining board, where May had left them to dry.

I could stab them. They would not feel anything if I stabbed them through the heart; it would be quick. The knives were sharp.

I need to stop thinking these thoughts. It's nonsense, I am not a killer. I am a good husband, a good father.

Then my father's voice came into my head. "No, you are not," he said. "You cannot even provide for them. Selling my tractor to feed them and give them presents? You are not a man."

This is where my story will end. I have taken the decision to hang myself. It will be painless for me and there will be no mess for May to clear up. The family are better off without me. I have failed them, and they need a stronger person to provide for them. I am a failure. I am going to leave a note for May and then go out into the barn. I have a strong rope and a suitable beam to perform the deed. If I stack up hay bales, I can kick them away and it will be quick and silent.

Chapter 14 – The Suicide Note: May's Account

Now that I have found the memoirs that Clifford has been writing, I have decided to continue the story so that one day, this account of his life can be read by anyone who is suffering depression and alcoholism. I do not want anyone to go through the pain and suffering that I am feeling. It has been three months since I found Clifford and I am using these writings to ease the pain.

On January 1st 1974, I awoke to the back door banging. It was cold in the house and I put on my dressing gown and went into the kitchen. Stuck to the table with a kitchen knife was a note. It was written in Clifford's handwriting and was very short:

"I am sorry, I love you and the children with all my heart, but you deserve better. A better man will provide for you. Do not go into the barn. Call the emergency services. Love, Clifford."

I ignored the note and went immediately to the barn, expecting to see Clifford with a shotgun, as I had found him years before. I did not expect him to have killed himself. He was suffering major headaches and was not coping, but he would not commit suicide. It is this decision I now regret. I should have called the emergency services.

The barn door was closed. This was unusual as it was never closed. I opened the door and saw Clifford hanging from the main beam. He was clearly dead. I screamed and, as I ran towards him, I felt another presence in the barn. I turned around and at the door was Fred. He was staring at his father's hanging body.

I stopped immediately and turned to him. "Get out!" I screamed at him, but he stood transfixed. His legs would not move; he just stood there, not saying a word, his eyes not blinking, wide open with terror. I ran to him and pushed him out of the barn, closing the door behind me.

"Dad's dead, isn't he?" Fred cried. I sat him down on the grass and told him that he should never have seen his father hanging. No child should see their father commit suicide. If only I had listened to Clifford in his final message, Fred would not have seen an image which would live with him for the rest of his life. No matter what I did in later years, he would have nightmares forever.

I sat with him on the grass and hugged him, both of us crying. Our lives were never to be the same again. My husband, who had gone to Christmas Island with no illnesses and had returned with major problems, was dead. I was alone with two children and a farm to run and I needed to mourn.

I called the police and told them what had happened. The note remained on the kitchen table. I shut the door to the kitchen, took both children into the front room of the house and sat them down. I explained to Fred and Elizabeth that their dad was dead. I told them that he had taken his own life due to his headaches. This was the hardest conversation that I have ever had. Telling your children that their father was dead is bad enough, but to tell them that he had killed himself is even worse.

The police arrived, and an ambulance. They treated the farm like a crime scene. The barn was taped off, the suicide note was bagged, and the house was dusted for fingerprints. I felt like a criminal, even though the police officer in charge was very sympathetic and tried to help me. I had no one. Both my parents were dead. Clifford's parents were dead. The only person I had was Clifford's brother, Ian, who I realised I had forgotten to call. The police told Ian and he came immediately to the house. We had never really got on, but that day, he hugged me and was my rock.

Clifford's body was removed from the barn and a post mortem was carried out. He had taken his own life, which meant our small life insurance policy did not pay out. I now had to find money to pay for his funeral. He had left no instructions and I knew no one in the Royal Navy, so we arranged for a small family ceremony and a cremation. I scattered his ashes on David's grave. He was now at peace.

It was while I was going through his artefacts that I found these memoirs. The children had gone to bed and I sat and read through his account of his life and the struggles he had faced. If only he had talked to me, we would have got through it. Why did he feel he was alone? Why could he not talk to me until it was too late?

Perhaps I had concentrated too much on the children. I had always stayed strong for them. David's death had caused major trauma within the family and I had struggled to cope with it. I then realised that I had not spoken to Clifford about any of my issues; I had got through it on my own. Our relationship had looked perfect to the outside world, but we had not talked through our problems. We each had our own demons and we had not tackled them together.

I cried whilst reading the papers. Clifford had tried his best but could not cope with the headaches and the exposure. He blamed himself for the children's problems and David's death. But it had not been his fault; it was the UK Government's fault. They sent him to the tests, they sent him up into the fallout, they were responsible. I decided that night to make sure that Clifford's life would not be forgotten. Even though he was now dead, I would not stop until he was officially recognised by the UK Government.

Chapter 15 – The Family Struggles

In 1975, I had to sell the farm. It was too big for us, the mortgage payments were high, and we were not farming the land. I needed a smaller house with lower running costs. This was my excuse.

The real reason was that every time I went into the kitchen, I saw the suicide note on the table, then I saw the barn through the window. I was struggling to cope with the images that filled my mind every day.

Fred had also retreated into himself. His promising football career had stalled; he was no longer playing for the county, he was not training, and he spent most of his time in his room. He refused to go into the barn for anything, he was becoming withdrawn and the arguments had started.

Elizabeth was struggling with her eyesight. Her friends were playing hockey, sewing and starting to take an interest in boys. She felt that she was not pretty. No boy had asked her out and she blamed her eye problem. "Who wants to go out with a blind person?" she would say, crying and running to her room.

I needed to change the family situation and a new house would begin the whole process. A fresh start for the three of us. It was strange saying "the three of us" as, two years ago, it was "the five of us". How had this happened? What had I done to deserve this?

The farm was sold, and we moved into a small three-bedroom terraced house in Salisbury. The children remained at their school and kept their friends. We sold a lot of furniture and I managed to purchase the house outright, so I had no mortgage. We had started a new life.

Elizabeth visited the doctor's as her eyesight had deteriorated. She needed a further operation. How was I going to cope with sending her to London and looking after Fred? Luckily, a family friend took Elizabeth to London and stayed with her whilst she had her operation. I could not be with her; it was one of the hardest things to do. I was split between the two children. I needed to work to pay the bills and I could not afford to take a week off work. With one income, money was tight. Even with no mortgage, the basic bills still needed to be paid.

On August 4th 1975, I put Elizabeth on the train to London with Stephen (our family friend) and they waved us goodbye. I smiled as she left the platform and then returned to my car, where I burst into tears. Another new start was turning into a nightmare. Each time we rebooted our lives, another problem would try and de-rail us. Stephen had strict instructions to call us every day at 6pm. However, we did not have a telephone, so I had to wait at the telephone box at the end of the street.

Stephen was true to his word and telephoned every day for five days. Elizabeth's operation had been a success and she was coming home. At last, some positive news. I waited on the platform at Salisbury train station for Elizabeth's train, Fred at my side. When her train arrived, she stepped off holding a white cane. She would need to use it for the rest of her life. She was 15 and, even though the operation had been a partial success, she was now registered blind.

To see your 15-year-old daughter rely on a white stick so she doesn't trip over or bump into objects is heart-breaking. She was so pretty; she had her whole life in front of her. The doctors did not know how long her remaining vision would last as she now only had 20% sight. Elizabeth took it in her stride. She asked for a guide dog and we applied to Guide Dogs for the Blind. Unfortunately, her sight was still too good for her to qualify, but it would only be a matter of time.

The Royal National Institute for the Blind provided the white cane and helped us with other adaptations (magnifying glasses etc.) so she could try and lead a normal life. Elizabeth was determined to go back to her mainstream school and after a few weeks recuperating at home, she returned to her classmates.

We struggled to make ends meet. We lived on benefits and my wages from working in the local shop. I was not qualified to undertake a well-paid job. In the evenings, I would take in ironing from the village and try to earn as much as possible. I was exhausted all the time.

Fred and Elizabeth continued to do well at school. Fred still suffered nightmares, when he would wake up in a cold sweat, screaming. I knew he was still seeing the image of his father hanging in the barn.

Elizabeth studied hard. Even though her eyesight was poor, she used a magnifying glass to read her school books. I tried to help her as much as possible and we converted the downstairs dining room into her bedroom so she did not have to use the stairs.

Fred was growing into a handsome young man. Tall and dark, he looked exactly like his father. He was back playing football and competing at county level. We were starting to live as a family again. I was not dating anyone; my whole life was dedicated to the children and providing for them. They were my life.

In 1978 Elizabeth was awarded a scholarship to university. She desperately wanted to study nuclear physics and learn about the mechanics and exposure risks. This was ironic as, at the time, she was unaware of the levels of radiation her father had been exposed to.

Her scholarship was to be in the USA at Harvard. It was such a long way to go, she was registered blind and I was worried. I could not afford to visit her, and she would only return once a year during the summer holidays.

We sat down as a family and decided she should go. It was her dream. In August 1978, a representative of the university met us at Heathrow Airport and escorted her to America. It was the start of a journey that I believed would allow her to put her terrible experiences to good use and enable the family to move on to a new chapter.

I missed her terribly. We were so close, and I was worried that she would not be able to cope with the demands of the course because of her disability. I decided to have a telephone installed which would allow me to talk to her and we communicated once a week for 10 minutes as calls were expensive at that time. Sunday evenings at 7pm. I looked forward to these conversations and when I spoke to her, she seemed to be enjoying the experience and was so full of life.

During 1978, Fred was getting attention from football clubs. His county manager had put him forward for trials with various professional clubs and it seemed as if his talent for football would allow him to escape his demons.

He attended a trial for Swindon Town in January 1979. It was a cold, frosty day and the pitch was hard. I watched as he went through his warm up with the other potential players and he looked so determined. The match was intense; competition for places was fierce. Fred scored a goal and was playing well. The other parents remarked that he had the talent to go far.

In the second half, Fred was tackled whilst running in on goal. It was not a nasty tackle, just a late one. He screamed and fell to the floor. The staff immediately went to help him. I was sure he would be OK. They carried him off the pitch and I went to his side. His left knee was very swollen, and he was in excruciating pain.

We were taken by ambulance to the hospital in Swindon, where doctors looked at his injury and initially told us he had torn ligaments. The swelling would subside, and he would be able to return to training in 6-8 weeks. Fred was upset, but as the injury was not substantial, it was good news.

We returned home, and the swelling did subside, but the pain in his knee didn't. We returned to the doctor and he organised a scan to see what the issue was. We waited for the scan for weeks and when the day came, Fred could still not walk without crutches.

His knee was scanned, and we were told that the results would be made available in two weeks. I had not told Elizabeth of Fred's injury as I did not want her to worry.

We visited the doctor's with Fred still unable to walk properly. The doctor asked us to sit down and told me that he had looked at the scan and was puzzled by the results. The scan showed that Fred had the bone density of a 70-year-old. He was only 16. The doctor asked lots of questions relating to Fred's health and his early life. He could not understand why this condition had happened and had gone undiagnosed for such a long time.

I asked Fred to wait in the waiting room whilst I discussed his father's exposure on Christmas Island with the doctor. I did not want Fred to know about the levels of radiation his father had been exposed to. The doctor was initially dismissive of any connection, but you could tell he was interested in the possible link.

The diagnosis was devastating for Fred. His career as a footballer was over. He would never be able to play football again and needed an operation on his knee.

Fred was inconsolable for the next few weeks. How could this be happening again? Why were we still suffering the effects of the nuclear testing programme? I was convinced there was a link between the tests and the children's conditions. I had believed that Fred was the lucky one without any major issues, but I was wrong. His bones were crumbling, and he would not live without pain for the rest of his life.

Fred refused to admit that he had any problems and was determined to continue to play football. He tried to build up the strength in his knee following the operation, but it was no use; his body was failing him. His talent was there, but his condition meant he could not fulfil his potential.

To watch your 16-year-old son try and fail and be unable to help him is extremely hard. We now had to find him a career and a new way forward. His condition limited what he could do, so we had to rethink his life. Again, the fallout of the bomb continued to affect our lives.

Elizabeth returned home for the summer of 1979. She had completed her first year at university and was excelling in her field. She was in the top 10% of her class. I was astounded to see her when we collected her from the airport. She had changed so much in the year; she was more confident, and she was enjoying her life in the USA.

During the summer, Fred talked a lot with his sister about his future. He wanted to join the navy like his father, but his condition meant he would not pass a medical. He was good with figures, so he decided to train to become an accountant. It was not going to be the glamorous lifestyle of a footballer, but it would put a roof over his head and pay his bills.

Fred studied hard and was awarded a place at Reading University. He left in 1981 and for the first time I was alone in the house. Elizabeth had another year before her studies finished and I did not know if she would return to the UK. It was at this time that I felt my lowest. I was still working, but my life no longer had a purpose. My children had grown up and they were embarking on their lives. I should be enjoying time with my husband. We had provided for our children and now it was time to relax and enjoy life, but I couldn't.

Coming home to an empty house, cooking for one and watching TV was my daily routine. I needed an escape. I decided that I would volunteer at a local animal shelter. I loved dogs, but as I still worked full time, I could not have one, so I put my time to good use, dog walking and helping in the shelter shop.

Christmas 1981 was very lonely. Fred had a girlfriend at university and decided to spend the holidays with her family in London. Elizabeth could not afford to return home, so I was alone at Christmas for the first time ever. I awoke on Christmas Day and drove to the cemetery. I sat and talked to David and Clifford for hours. It was cold, but there were lots of other people visiting and a number of people talked to me.

I was invited to a New Year's Eve party with the volunteers from the animal shelter and I decided to go and let my hair down. It was at this party that I met Jeff. He was a retired solicitor and was also passionate about dogs.

I started 1982 with a new passion and someone to spend time with. I no longer needed to be on my own. Jeff and I started to see more of each other, but I could not go further than friends. My husband was the love of my life and I could not commit to anyone else.

Elizabeth graduated with honours. I was extremely proud. I had saved enough money to attend her graduation and Fred and I flew to the USA to watch her collect her degree. It was the proudest moment of my life. My daughter had overcome her disability and had come through it. She was a graduate with a degree in nuclear physics.

The trip to the USA made Fred even more determined to pass his degree. "I am doing it for Dad," he said to me on the flight home. "If Elizabeth can do it, so can I." He was determined to pass.

Elizabeth returned home and looked for work, eventually finding a job with the UK Atomic Energy Authority (UKAEA). She had to re-locate to Abingdon, Oxfordshire but she was happy and enjoying her new role.

1983 saw Jeff and me get serious for the first time. Elizabeth told me to move on with my life. "We will never forget Dad," she said, "but we must move on." Jeff was a caring, educated, well-dressed man who shared my passions. We became a couple but did not move in together. We still lived apart but spent more and more time together.

Fred was settled at university and was happy with his long-term girlfriend. He was due to graduate in 1984. And I was happy at last, too. Jeff and I enjoyed romantic dinners, walks with the dogs, trips abroad and he spoilt me with presents.

It was at this time that I became aware of the British Nuclear Test Veterans Association (BNTVA). I contacted the founder, Mr Ken McGinley, who told me that I was not alone. Thousands of veterans had returned with illnesses and their children had health problems. A pattern was emerging. Jeff encouraged me to keep in contact with the association and to ensure that we never forgot Clifford.

I spent the summer of 1983 in Cyprus with Jeff. We had a wonderful time. The weather was hot and for once I was under no stress or pressure. Jeff had a successful solicitor's practice and was still a director, taking a salary. He was very wealthy, and for the first time in my life I did not need to worry about money.

In 1984, Fred graduated from university with a first-class honours degree. Elizabeth, Jeff and I attended the ceremony. After the ceremony, Fred asked me to drive him to Salisbury cemetery as he wanted to show his father that he had achieved his goals. He asked to be dropped off and picked up an hour later. I knew this was something he had to do alone, so I left him at the graveside of his father.

I do not know what he talked about; I am sure he just wanted to show his father his degree and to make him proud. I have never asked him what he did for the hour he was alone. It is his business and if he wants to tell me, he will.

Fred returned home to Salisbury and I made the decision to move in with Jeff. We kept our house in Salisbury and Fred was to live in it. It was his and Elizabeth's legacy and I was glad that I was able to help him in his career.

Chapter 16 – May's Fight with the Government and BNTVA Help

In 1985, I contact the BNTVA and asked for their help. Jeff had been doing some research and he was convinced I was due a war pension. We needed to prove that Clifford's death was due to his service and his exposure to the radiation.

The BNTVA were fantastic. They helped me with the application and, using Jeff's research, we filed a claim. We waited for a response for months. In May 1985 I received a letter from the government rejecting my application. There was insufficient evidence to prove that Clifford had taken his own life as a result of the radiation exposure.

Jeff was incensed. This was a cover up! How could they deny the exposure? We decided to apply to the MoD for Clifford's service and medical records. Jeff did all the paperwork. After a few months, his medical records were delivered, but there was nothing in there relating to the psychiatric sessions he had undertaken. Those documents were missing.

We complained, and, after two further attempts, we were finally sent the records. Within the records there was also a document with Clifford's dosimeter readings. We had the evidence to prove that he had been irradiated.

We appealed the first decision and presented the new evidence. I received a holding letter, informing me that the appeal committee would meet to discuss my case.

It was in October 1985 that I received a letter informing me that my appeal had been successful, and I had been awarded a pension. We had finally won recognition for Clifford. This small amount of money that I was to be paid every month would help Fred and Elizabeth. I set up a special account for them and paid the money directly into it.

Without the help of the BNTVA, I would never have received a pension from the UK Government. It had never occurred to me that there would be an organisation for the nuclear veterans. I had seen lots of navy charities, but never considered looking for a nuclear veterans-based organisation.

I received six payments from the government and then received a letter informing me that, following a review, the payments were to stop as I was no longer eligible. Surely this was a mistake? How could I no longer be eligible? My circumstances hadn't changed. Jeff was very angry. The time and effort spent on the application was significant and now, for the payments to stop without warning ... Something was wrong.

Again with the help of the BNTVA, we appealed the decision. I was told I needed to attend a hearing in London of the appeal committee, which would decide whether the payments would resume. I asked the BNTVA to represent me and they agreed.

In June 1986, Jeff and I, along with a representative of the BNTVA, attended the hearing. The committee went into Clifford's childhood and upbringing and tried to say that my husband was not of sound body and mind before he left for Christmas Island. Luckily for me, Jeff was a trained solicitor and had prepared evidence to the contrary.

The independent judge heard the evidence and ruled in our favour. We were awarded more money than in the previous claim and the payments were backdated. We had fought the government for a second time and won.

I was exhausted. The hearing lasted for two days and even though we won, I could not help but think that we should not even need to fight for this justice. Why were the government denying any responsibility for the effects on these veterans? What were they hiding?

I was contacted by a representative of the MoD and asked where I had obtained the documentation with Clifford's dosimeter readings. When I told him the MoD had sent me the information he was flabbergasted. I am sure he did not believe me. I knew then that they had the readings and documents on all participants at the tests, but they were not prepared to release them.

Chapter 17 – A Quick Update

I have not written in these memoirs for a long time because my life has been extremely good. Jeff and I have never married but continue to live together happily. We have both lost partners and feel that there is no need to marry each other. I am now 68 and have retired from work.

Jeff is 70 and still very fit and healthy. I feel very lucky to have met him and lived a new life with him. It is as if my life was in two parts: with Clifford, and after Clifford. I sometimes sit and think of Clifford and how different my life would have been.

Fred and Elizabeth still live in the house in Salisbury. Fred is a qualified accountant and has never married – I believe because he is frightened he may pass on health issues to any children. His bones continue to deteriorate, and he now walks with a stick.

Elizabeth has only 10% of her sight remaining. Living with Fred has helped her; he looks after her and ensures she is cared for. They have employed a housekeeper, who cooks and cleans the house, as their health conditions mean they are unable to perform these tasks themselves.

Elizabeth has regular checks on her eyes. She is now completely blind in her left eye and she is due to have a false eye fitted in 2007. I worry that she will go totally blind. She has a guide dog called Ben who is her world. He helps her immensely and I believe that without Ben she would not be able to cope with life. She still manages to work from home and is busy preparing research documents, but she is not very mobile.

My main concern is for Fred, for he is becoming a recluse. He has no social life; he prepares accounts from home and hardly leaves the house. Food is delivered, and he rarely visits me. I message him a lot and he replies, but when I ask him to visit, he always has some excuse. I think he may have agoraphobia.

I visit as much as possible. My children are grown adults, but they are still my children. I visit David's grave regularly and often sit and talk to him and Clifford and ask them what they are doing. David was my eldest child and I believe that he would have been the one to give me grandchildren. As neither Fred or Elizabeth have any children, the family name is going to die with them. This makes me sad. They both chose not to have children. They have not told me why, but I believe they discussed it and made the decision together.

Chapter 18 – Further Health Issues

In November 2006, I found a lump in my breast and went to the doctor's. I was immediately taken for a scan and they found a cancerous tumour. I decided to have a mastectomy. It was a difficult decision. Jeff fully supported me, and I underwent surgery in December 2006. My recovery was difficult. I felt that I was no longer a woman. Jeff told me not to be so silly: he loved me, and he would be there for me.

I underwent reconstructive surgery in 2007 and felt well. Fred and Elizabeth were very supportive. They came to visit me in hospital and I was extremely grateful that they made the effort. It took Fred a lot of courage to leave the house and I could see he was struggling. The following months were spent with follow up appointments and in 2008 I was given the all clear.

In February 2009, Elizabeth was rushed to hospital. She had gone blind. Fred telephoned me in a panic. His agoraphobia was so bad that he could not even get in the ambulance with his sister. He was at home, and was distraught. I calmed him down and rushed to the hospital to be with Elizabeth. We had known this day would come, but I had hoped that she would have more years of sight.

When I arrived at the hospital, she was sitting up in bed. Her eyes looked swollen and painful, but when I held her hand, she smiled and said, "It has finally happened. I had a good run at it, didn't I, Mum?"

She was in good spirits, but I did not know what to say. I asked the specialists if they could help. They told me they would need to do further tests, but at present there was nothing they could do. Her sight would not return.

I telephoned Fred and assured him that his sister was OK and he was not to panic. She would be staying in hospital for a few days and we needed to prepare the house for her return.

Whilst I was visiting Elizabeth I received a telephone call from the police. They told me that Clifford's brother Ian had been rushed into hospital – the same hospital where I was sitting with my daughter. I went to the emergency room and was told that Ian had suffered a heart attack and died in the ambulance.

The day could not get any worse. Ian and I had remained close and on numerous occasions I had visited the family farm, where he had continued to tend the land. His wife had died in 2000 and they had no children. I was his only family.

I now had a sick child and a funeral to arrange. I telephoned Jeff, who immediately came to the hospital and handled Ian's affairs. I was too involved with Elizabeth and her illness to arrange a funeral and sort out the paperwork needed for Ian.

Elizabeth returned home four days later, although she would need further tests. Jeff had discovered Ian's will. He had left the farm to my children. Elizabeth and Fred were his sole heirs. I informed them, and they immediately decided that they would like to live on the farm. Fred wanted the seclusion and Elizabeth needed the space of the farmhouse.

We buried Ian next to his wife and brother in the same cemetery as David and Clifford. Fred did not attend the funeral; he could not leave the house, even for such an occasion. Elizabeth did attend; with the help of her guide dog Ben she was coping with her blindness.

We decided to sell the house in Salisbury and pay for adaptations to the farmhouse. The house made a good profit and Elizabeth and Fred lived with Jeff and me until the farmhouse was finished. Jeff oversaw the changes and project managed the adaptations.

In June 2008, Fred and Elizabeth moved into the farmhouse. The adaptations allowed them to have separate spaces, but they could help each other in the kitchen and living rooms. A housekeeper was employed full time and they were well looked after.

Fred enjoyed the seclusion; the farm was set off the road and no one came to visit apart from deliveries and family. The barn in which their father had taken his own life was visible from the land but it did not seem to bother the children.

I was happy to see my children back on the family farm. They were content with their lives and everything was back on track.

Chapter 19 – Terminal Diagnosis

Life carried on. Jeff and I were happy. Our lifestyles were changing due to age, but we remained active and continued to volunteer at the animal shelter.

Elizabeth and Fred lived in the farmhouse and we had now rented the land to a farmer, which provided much-needed income. Elizabeth had lost her guide dog Ben to cancer and she had not replaced him. As she did not leave the confines of the farm, she didn't feel she needed another dog. She always told me that someone else who was more in need than her should have a dog.

She had Fred and the live-in housekeeper and that was all she needed. She had learnt braille and was reading braille books, listening to the radio and watching TV for the soundtrack. I do not know how she stayed so positive.

Fred was now walking with two sticks; his crumbling body was slowly deteriorating. I visited the farm and took them homemade jams and cake. He looked like an 80-year-old. The young boy who had so much talent for football now looked like an old man.

These frequent visits to the farmhouse always made me happy until we left. The driveway to the farm swept around the back of the house and I always saw the barn on the neighbour's land where Clifford had committed suicide. The image of him hanging from the beam was always the last image I had when leaving the farm.

Life moved on. We spent Christmas at the farm, as Fred would not travel, and we were a happy family. I worried about the children, but they supported each other, and they seemed to be content with their lives.

In January 2016, I felt pains in my chest. I put it down to old age and despite Jeff's best efforts, I did not arrange a doctor's appointment. However, by March, I knew something was wrong. Jeff insisted that I make an appointment with the doctor. He told me I needed a scan, but he believed that my cancer had returned. I had the symptoms; he just wanted to ensure his diagnosis was correct.

I underwent a full MRI scan in April 2016; Jeff paid for a private scan. The doctor's diagnosis was confirmed. My cancer had returned, and it had spread to other areas of my body. I was given 12 months to live.

Jeff was devastated. He would not accept that I was going to die and he was angry at the diagnosis. There had been so much death in the family already. Why did such sadness seem to hang over our family like a cloud? However, I accepted the diagnosis. I was 79 years old and I had been very lucky to have met Jeff. He had saved me from depression and we had spent a lot of wonderful years together.

Jeff wanted me to try chemotherapy and any new treatments, but I did not want to. I accepted my illness and wanted to enjoy myself in the time I had left. I created a bucket list and Jeff and I started on the list. Trips to Africa to see the animals, to Niagara Falls and to Egypt.

Fred and Elizabeth sensed there was something wrong, but I did not want to tell them until nearer the end. I did not want to put any stress on their already fragile lives.

By December 2016 I was too ill to travel and complete my bucket list. It was time to tell the children. I wanted one last Christmas, as I had had with David, and I wanted it to be fun. Telling your children that you have months to live is hard, especially when they have already suffered so much pain in their lives. They have seen so much death: their brother, father, grandmother, uncle and now their mother.

We decided that Jeff and I would give them the news on December 28th. I was now very ill, but I was determined we would spend Christmas together as a family and enjoy the day. Jeff drove us to the farm and we spent the day opening presents, playing board games and watching TV. By 4pm, I was so tired that we decided to stay overnight with Elizabeth and Fred. Fred was worried about me, but I said I had the flu.

In fact, Jeff and I decided to stay at the farm until New Year's Day, when we would return home. On the morning of the 28th, I told the children I only had months to live. They were devastated. Elizabeth began to sob uncontrollably, and Fred just came and hugged me.

Fred told me that he wanted me to stay with him until the end. He wanted me to live with him, so he could look after me. I told him Jeff would look after me and that he did not want his mother to die at his home. He understood my reasons, but I could tell he was hurt and upset. I told him I would see in the new year with him.

We spent the holidays looking through old photos, laughing at the clothes I had made the children wear, the old-fashioned haircuts and makeup. Their father's time on Christmas Island was never mentioned. They knew he had been stationed there, but they never knew the lethal radiation levels he had been exposed to.

On New Year's Eve, we saw in the new year together. It took all my strength to stay up and write this. I've kept up with the memoirs because I did not want them to end. Fred and Elizabeth are part of this story and they need to know the full account of their father's life.

Chapter 20 – Fred's Account

Jeff gave me these memoirs after my mother died, on January 1st 2017. I knew nothing of the existence of these documents; she had managed to keep them secret from Elizabeth and me. We have decided that I will continue to update this memoir as it is an important part of our family story. One day I hope it will be published, and our story will help other nuclear veterans.

We buried Mum on 15th January in the same cemetery as my brother and father. Finally, they were back together.

Jeff continued to support us. He was a fantastic step-dad and without him, we would not have been able to survive. He was mourning for my mother and the spark seemed to fade a little when we saw him. He was always such a positive man, but he seemed to be lost. I tried to console him; I have experienced so much death in my life that I feel I am an expert.

Elizabeth and I continue to live in the farmhouse. Mum had a life insurance policy that took care of us. We did not need to work and the benefits we received paid for the upkeep of the house. We no longer had a housekeeper; I took on that role as we could not afford to pay her.

I try and visit the cemetery as much as possible, but each day I find it harder to leave the house. Elizabeth needs help with basic tasks and my spine is not coping with the lifting I am now doing.

In March 2017, a police car approached the farmhouse. I knew there was a problem when two uniformed officers came to the door. "We need to speak to Fred Jones," they said. "I am afraid we have bad news. Jeff Keeper has been found dead at home. We believe he suffered a heart attack."

I couldn't believe this was happening. Two months after my mum died, Jeff could not be dead as well. I was taken by the police to identify his body. I had to summon up as much strength as possible to leave the house. A police liaison officer stayed with Elizabeth.

At the hospital, I was taken into a room where, lying on a bed, was a body with a sheet over it. The sheet was raised, and I was asked to identify Jeff.

I was taken back to the farm by the police. Elizabeth asked me if I was sure it was him and I told her it was definitely Jeff. A post mortem was undertaken. Jeff had suffered a massive coronary due to ischaemic heart disease. The official death certificate confirmed it. But Elizabeth and I both knew he'd died of a broken heart. He could not live without Mum.

Jeff had arranged everything in his will – funds for the funeral, the hymns, his burial plot – so Elizabeth and I did not have to worry about anything. Once again, we were sole heirs. Jeff had left us everything.

His funeral was a small ceremony. Apart from Elizabeth and me, only 15 people attended. It was a very sad day. He was buried next to my mother.

The next few months were spent emptying Jeff's house and selling it. He had requested the house be sold, and a trust fund set up for Elizabeth and me so we were cared for. This final act of kindness was something I never expected. He had taken us on as his own and even in death was providing for us. I could not help thinking that he had provided more for us than our own father.

Chapter 21 – Help for Elizabeth

In the months that followed, Elizabeth became withdrawn and depressed. She told me that she had nothing to live for: she could not work, she had no children, there was no legacy. Our parents were dead and she could not see why she should continue with her life.

I could see the signs of depression. I had been through the same feelings and did not want her to experience them. I called a doctor to the house and he prescribed anti-depressants, but she refused to take them. She stopped eating and spent her day either in bed or on the settee in the lounge. She was just existing. She needed a purpose, something to live for.

I contacted the Samaritans and asked them for advice. They told me she needed to get professional help for her condition, that she needed to see a specialist. I arranged for a specialist to visit the farm, but she refused to see him. She was retreating into herself.

I decided to be tough with her. I made us a meal and told her to sit at the table and that we were to discuss what we were going to do. I became convinced that she wanted to die. I could not let her die; she was the only family I had left. I would not be able to live without her. We needed each other.

I contacted a private psychiatric unit and arranged for Elizabeth to be transferred by private ambulance to their facility in North Wales. Elizabeth needed help for her severe depression, and her blindness needed special care. The clinic was not cheap, and it would use a lot of the funds that Jeff had left us, but Elizabeth was worth it.

Elizabeth spent the next four months at the clinic and made good progress. I, however, found the months very lonely and my depression started to return. My mind kept wandering to the day in the barn when I saw my father hanging from the beam.

I started taking anti-depressants and when the clinic telephoned me and told me that Elizabeth was well enough to come home, I did not know if I could cope. I was happy that she was well enough to return, but I did not know if I was strong enough.

Elizabeth returned in November 2017 and we spent Christmas together, just the two of us. I took her to the cemetery to visit the family and she placed wreaths on the graves of our family members. We were the only family left.

In early 2018, my health took a turn for the worse. My spine was so bad that I was in constant pain and could not lift or do any housework. Social Services advised us that we needed to seek help and maybe it was time to sell the farm and move into specialist housing, where carers could help with our needs.

We were not old in age, but we had so many issues that we needed to make a decision. Elizabeth did not want to leave the farm, though. We could afford to live there, but if anything happened to one of us, could the other cope?

We decided to give it six months and review our situation. If we were coping then we would stay; if not, we would sell the farm and move into more suitable accommodation.

The summer of 2018 was an extremely hot one and we spent a lot of time sitting outside. I read to Elizabeth: she liked to keep up with news of nuclear developments and the nuclear veterans. We listened to audio books and she seemed to be content.

Chapter 22 – The Accident

It was during one of those hot nights that I decided we needed a cup of coffee before we went to bed. I entered the kitchen and fell over the Hoover, which I had left out. It was a stupid accident – I should have put the Hoover away – but I fell and hit my head on the corner of the table and knocked myself out.

I do not know how long I was on the floor. I was awoken by paramedics. Elizabeth had called for me when I hadn't returned with the coffee and had come to find me. She had also tripped over the Hoover and landed on me. Luckily, she had not banged her head and she was able to call 999.

I refused hospital treatment as I needed to ensure that Elizabeth was safe. If I went to hospital, no one would be there to look after her. I thought I had suffered concussion, because I had headaches for days afterwards.

The headaches continued into the next month and I found myself visiting the doctor. An MRI scan was performed on my head and I was given the news that I had a brain tumour. The tumour was inoperable, and I had between three and six months to live. If I had not tripped over, I would never have found out.

How was I going to tell Elizabeth? She was never going to survive without care. She needed me; I could not die and leave her. When I returned from the doctor's, she knew something was wrong because I was withdrawn and sad. I told her the truth and she cried and cried. We were the only surviving members of the family and we needed each other.

We decided to put our affairs in order, to prepare these memoirs and ensure that our story was up to date. I was following the BNTVA and had seen the publication of a new book. We decide that we would contact the author and ask him to publish our story.

Elizabeth and I fell into deep depressions. We started drinking heavily and I started nightly visits to the barn. I don't know why I started to visit the barn after all these years; I guess I wanted to put any ghosts to rest before I passed on.

I sat in the barn staring at the beam, the image of my father hanging there in my mind, my mother's horror at seeing me and how she closed the door and put me first before her feelings. I do not know how she did it.

At the time, I had not known why my father had committed suicide and I always wondered why he chose that moment. After reading these memoirs, I know that he killed himself to protect us. His headaches were so severe that he could not cope. I firmly believe that he would have killed us all if he had not taken his own life.

His death did have a major impact on my life, but I now see him as a hero. He fought for his country, did his duty and was left to die by his own government. He was betrayed and, as a family, we have also been betrayed. The suffering of my family because of the nuclear testing programme cannot be ignored. This story needs to be told.

Sixty years after my father attended the tests, we are still living in the shadow of the bomb. My sister and I suffer daily from multiple problems. The BNTVA are looking for medal recognition and I hope they get it. It is too late for my father and mother, but there are surviving veterans who should be recognised. I have just seen a Facebook post about an All Tests Reunion at Weston-Super-Mare. The trustees of the BNTVA are doing a fantastic job and everyone at the reunion seems to be enjoying themselves.

The new memorial at the National Memorial Arboretum will be a fitting tribute to the veterans and their families. My father would be proud of the work that the charities representing the nuclear veterans are doing.

My sister and I are living day to day. We have good days and bad days, but we want to help in the fight for recognition. I have sent these memoirs to Slaine McRoth with strict instructions to edit and publish them and to give the profits to the BNTVA, who helped my mother when she needed it.

I do not know how long my sister and I have; my diagnosis is not good. I might make it to the end of the year, but I am on borrowed time.

My sister is my main concern and I have ensured that when I die, she is well looked after in a specialist care facility. She is unaware of these arrangements, but I will die knowing she is safe.

I have made my funeral arrangements and will be buried in the same cemetery as my family. I have also reserved a plot for Elizabeth, so she does not have to worry. My father always told me to provide for my family. In a way he did provide for us; he left us too young, but our family survived. This is something that I will ensure happens for Elizabeth. The Jones name will die with me, but the memory of my father, my mother and my siblings will live on in these documents. I hope they are published and can raise some funds to help the remaining veterans and their families.

I will forever live in the shadow of the bomb.
Fred

Addendum by Slaine McRoth

Elizabeth contacted me to say that Frederick died on 10th October 2018. She could not find him in the morning and called for assistance. When the paramedics arrived, they searched the house and could not find him either.

They found him in the barn, hanging from the same beam as his father. He had taken his own life, aged 56. Elizabeth is preparing to be moved into a care facility where her needs can be met. Fred arranged everything before his death. He left this suicide note:

Dearest Elizabeth,

I do not want to be a burden on you as I battle this brain tumour. I will be leaving you knowing that you will be cared for and will not have to worry about anything. Our father always told us to work hard and to ensure the family was looked after. I hope that I have achieved this. I am at peace now with Mum, Dad and David.

Please do not mourn me. We had some good times. I wanted to thank you for everything you did for me. I love you. Please take care and enjoy a happy life. We will be watching over you.

Frederick.

Elizabeth still wants this memoir published. She is adamant that this extremely sad story should be put to good use to help the veterans in their fight for medal recognition. She hopes that a children's study will be undertaken by the UK Government to collate evidence of the families' suffering to be used to ensure the nuclear veterans no longer have to continue to fight. She also hopes that other veterans and their families who have experienced physical and mental health problems will read this story and know they are not alone. They have a voice in Fallout and the BNTVA.

All profits from this book will go to the BNTVA.

Personally, until recently I did not know much about the British nuclear test veterans, their families and their continuing struggle. There have been so many deaths, so many physical and mental health problems and the UK Government refuses to recognise this. In fact, it chooses to fight the veterans. Now that I have published these two books, I will continue to help the BNTVA as much as possible. Their story is one that needs to be told to every human being alive today.

All profits from this book will go to
The British Nuclear Test Veterans Association
www.bntva.com

The X, Y and Z Files: The 100-Year Experiment

This is the story of Sir James Gordon Josephson, OBE as he recalls his life as a civil servant monitoring the British nuclear tests of the 1950s and 1960s.

Hear about his unique life and gain insights into the testing programme and the British government's denial of any exposure to its servicemen.

His story is one which defies belief and one you must read. No longer can the secrets be withheld from the servicemen and their families.

50% of profits from sales of this book will be donated to the British Nuclear Test Veterans Association

Available in paperback and on Kindle